I0604091

None of the characters or references or places are meant to represent any person living or dead, or any particular place. None of the scenes ever took place, there is no association with anything beyond the writer's imagination.

ISBN 978-0-9989004-1-4
Washington Street Press
New York, NY, USA
washingtonstreetpress.com
2025

THIS IS WHAT I OWE YOU

A SHORT STORY

KRISTIN HART

*Ultimately one loves one's desires,
and not that which is desired.*
— Friedrich Nietzsche

THIS IS WHAT I OWE YOU

KRISTIN HART

"I just got released this afternoon."

Those were Jake's first words to me. They should have been an ample warning: he was too stupid even to lie. Not fresh out of jail, it turned out, but a psychiatric hospital, which unfortunately roused my interest. We were drinking 7&7's in the bar at a motel by the freeway. I was eager to escape from one oppression and blind to one much worse, ready to bind up my fate with anybody willing to buy me a drink.

He proceeded to tell me the whole story. How he and his wife had developed a taste for cocaine and snorted it together every night for over a year. How she'd been systematically denying it since his arrest, how everyone believed her, how this drove him to despair. He even described how she spread cocaine on her cunt to make it numb and then forced him to lick it for hours. Could he have made that up? he wondered.

Did I believe him? That his wife had snorted cocaine too?

I said that sure. I believed him.

He described how one night near dawn she'd sent him out for cigarettes and beer. He'd returned to the driveway stuffing half a cheeseburger into his mouth with one hand and tucking the wrapper under his seat with the other, but then forgot to steer and skidded halfway through the neighbor's yard, dragging the mangled carcass of their golden retriever under his tires, bringing his marriage to an abrupt end.

From that moment she pretended not to recognize him. When the police arrived she told them he'd been abusing her and her teenage children and she was sick of him.

Because he had a good job with the phone company and was expensively insured, he was quickly rushed into a private rehabilitation center. His wife came only for group therapy, which she loved, but she refused to look at him and still denied she'd ever used cocaine. Instead she cried and got things off her chest and even diagnosed herself. She was relieved to learn that she'd been Jake's enabler.

In therapy he focused like a pit bull on her denial of cocaine, lost his temper repeatedly and made the implications of abuse seem very plausible. He worked himself into a suicidal frenzy, was tied up and sedated and moved into solitary, and when his insurance ran out was transferred to State Hospital, where divorce papers were quietly served.

There was something cruel and menacing about the way his eyes expanded and his nostrils flared while he was talking. This turned out to be the aftermath of a line of coke he'd just done in the bathroom, in truth there was nothing sadistic about him at all. But I had a misdirected inkling he might satisfy desires that I couldn't have entrusted to a smarter man, and so that night we shared a room, and three days later took an apartment nearby. He was 39 and already not aging gracefully. I was 19.

We were in the town's seediest bar, where I was still a stranger, when he described his plan to me. His idea of bringing up cocaine in court. I should have known that he was dumb enough to do it. But I hardly paid attention to him. He glanced in the mirror behind the bar, licked his palm and smoothed his hair, and with his eyes still locked on his own image he told me. He said it was perfect. After his wife had taken her oath he was going to stand, point at her dramatically, and demand she tell the truth. Thereby he would force her to admit she was a coke freak too.

His eyes turned to me. They were glistening.

I smiled, took a sip of my drink, and told him to accept the settlement.

Never! He would never let that bitch keep his TV and his sectional! They were top-of-the-line and the TV was only two months old, hardly watched, equipped with picture-in-the-picture. The sectional had a button to make it vibrate. And he was paying for them! No, never, he was fighting back! He would not accept the settlement with his tail between his legs, allow that whore to relax on his couch, flipping the channels, snorting cocaine with her boyfriend and laughing at him. He would have his day in court. He would force that bitch to show her colors. The truth would be victorious. He would see to that.

I smiled again and told him it was probably better not to mention cocaine in court.

He only shook his head and said he knew what he was doing. I took another drink, pulled an ice cube out and sucked on it, and asked what his lawyer thought of this plan.

"Well, baby, the lawyer worked for him! And if he wanted to fight, they'd fight."

I asked him to please stop calling me baby and explained that people didn't always tell the truth in court. I told him that, in fact, they lied routinely.

"It's not truth serum," I said.

But I couldn't believe I had to say this and was peering at him with a smile. The whole idea was a joke. Nobody would really do this. And besides, our little world was make believe. His smoldering face was merely an excuse to stay in bed. I was much more concerned with getting him to stop calling me baby. What absorbed me at that moment was the endless promise of a drink, those first few sips of whiskey on a summer afternoon, the hot white glare of a deserted main street, remembered when somebody new walked in and then forgotten like the underlying purpose of a dream.

And so even when I saw that he persisted, and day after day was perfecting his plan– he imagined himself standing, he imagined the raised eyebrows and sudden hush of the courtroom as they awaited what he'd say, saw the wife's prudish facade melt before their eyes, the truth triumphant, the big screen TV and the sectional returned to their rightful owner, the shaking of hands afterward, the wife scurrying toward the door in disgrace– even then I didn't take him seriously, but smiled and told him he'd already seen too much TV so he should let her keep the big screen. I was safe in a world where no one voluntarily interrupted simple divorce proceedings to utter the word cocaine– where there were lawyers to prevent this– where Jake was still a sexual promise about to be fulfilled– and where everything we said was an elaborate pretext for sex. And so when, eyes blazing, wiping the powder off his nose, he told me that he'd get his wife to publicly admit she'd used cocaine or he would kill her, I took a long drink, lay back, smiled up at him and spread my legs, pretending this hatred was for me.

I wasn't at all uneasy about the trial and was even looking forward to it. It sounded fun. I wanted a good long look at the wife. I'd already noticed the attention Jake and I attracted on the street, the double takes that withered me with shame, and I wanted to see another woman who had briefly thought he was acceptable. I wanted to sit in the back of the courtroom and watch Jake, in his only suit and brown knit tie, enter with his lawyer, a squirrely little man, elegantly dressed, with a face red and shiny as a polished apple. I liked pretending Jake was a stranger and sometimes did it for no particular reason. He became so completely unfamiliar, so fast, that for a long time I was unable to convince myself I knew him and even hours later remained pleasantly doubtful. I wanted to sit unnoticed far in the back, behind his buddy Bob Wickett– an unemployed Vietnam vet who lived with his mother (and an eyewitness! he'd seen the wife with snorting straw in hand) — behind Jake's elderly parents and his fat, mildly retarded teenager daughter who smiled all the time, behind the wife's girlfriends from the office and her own two teenage children, a boy and a girl, fat too but not officially retarded.

But Jake would not let me come to the trial.

How could the young girl he'd shacked up with be allowed to come to his divorce? I thought he was joking about this too. I tried to explain what I knew to be true– that no one would care– but he insisted I would hurt his case, and so I waited in the truck all afternoon, in the courthouse parking lot.

It was hot and I watched the police coming and going from a small gray building attached to the backside of the courthouse and I could hear their calculated whistling.

After two hours I started to feel nervous. I knew it shouldn't take this long. The marriage had only lasted a year and a half, and his prolonged absence now did not bode well. I had a premonition that I should get out of the truck and run to the freeway, on the lip of which this town grew like a cold sore, hitch a ride and get as far away as possible. But I never moved. My eyes were glued to the courthouse steps, where after about four hours the ex-wife finally appeared. She wore a pink dress and looked more and more naked the closer she got. She was a small woman, flanked on either side by a heavy blond teenager in black jeans and elaborate orthodontic headgear.

Then she recognized the truck, and saw me in it, and a smile of amusement crossed her face. For a moment I felt as if I was the truck, squatting obscenely in the nearly empty parking lot. He hadn't even left me with the keys. She was talking to a man in a corduroy suit, listening intently with a hand cupped on the side of her face against the sun. Now and then, when her eyes strayed to the truck, she smiled. She had a greasy orange face and cheeks that stood out from it like giant commas and a very bad perm and there were gold threads in the fabric of her dress and a gold belt cinched around a tidy waist. She shook hands with the man and walked right past me, smiling, stuffed her children into a white Grand Am and drove away.

For fifteen minutes nothing happened. Again I thought of fleeing. Then Jake stumbled out the door and stood at the top of the steps alone, peering at the brightness all around him. Where was the lawyer? Where were his parents? Where was Bob Wickett? He staggered toward me, moving so slowly across the parking lot that I smoked one entire cigarette and lit another. Then he was suddenly at the open window of the truck.

"Well, baby." There was a strange, feminine squeaking sound in his throat. His face was livid and his nostrils flared.

"Well, baby, I'm a free man," he said.

He collapsed against the side of the truck with a sob. For a moment I stayed where I was and through the chalky windshield watched a kid on a skateboard expertly surf the courthouse stairs and disappear around the corner.

Then I climbed out of the truck and crouched beside him.

"You're all I've got, baby," he moaned.

"Let me guess," I said. "You mentioned the cocaine."

It was a disaster. After a brief impassioned speech in support of the ex-wife, who was obviously traumatized, the judge made an exception to Michigan law and ordered alimony. Three hundred dollars a week to be taken directly from his wages for three years. The town shared a healthy laugh about this and forgot about him. But Jake's despair became a permanent condition, my love the only thing keeping him from suicide.

He had violent fits of self-directed rage. He might be cheerfully frying some eggs when suddenly he'd put his hand flat into the greasy pan until sizzled. He might punch himself in the chest as hard as he could without warning and then fall to the floor, gasping as if really injured. And what could I do but rush to him and tell him something calming? He was a big, hairy, fleshy man with cold damp skin and shoulders that sloped like an overburdened wire hanger. I rubbed his temples while the hysterics leveled into wheezing and then finally he dozed off and I stared down at the huge cragged face between my hands, its fluttering veiny eyelids, its half-open mouth and rotting teeth, and hated him.

I still hoped to get some satisfaction out of my entrapment. I hoped that he might understand my masochism. And he almost did. Everything was almost with him. His face was almost kind, almost marked with suffering, almost intelligent, his sadness almost touched me. But this approximate quality rendered him entirely nonthreatening, and he grew increasingly dense to my broad hints.

Finally, with the help of something he called crank– we could no longer afford cocaine– I told him what I wanted. And he attempted to comply. But these attempts were mortifying. He tied me to the bed so incompetently that I could have easily moved my hands and had to lie perfectly still trying not to shift my wrists.

Or he came at me swinging his penis around like a watch on a chain.

My heart sank, my frustration flourished, I hated him more and more. But instead of fleeing as I should have, as I'd planned to all along, I seemed to have already invested too much time and energy, too many painfully embarrassing instructions, and with the slightest bit more prodding, I thought, he might figure it out and comply.

And so I insisted more and more absurdly on my loyalty. I would not betray him– I was different– I was not like his ex-wife– I loved him. These tawdry promises, loosened by whisky, flowed from my mouth with frightening ease and he accepted them as natural and entirely his due. My words stared me in the face each morning, Jake already gone for work, which was futile, of course, all the money went to his ex-wife, but I preferred him gone and did not point this out, with nothing for me to do but sleep. It was a simple mistake but maybe I would stay forever, this hatred was a fact I had to live with. At half past four each afternoon I dragged myself into the shower and then guiltily got dressed. My body was always swollen and tender with sleep. When he got home at five we started drinking.

I spent half of every evening in the bathroom and remember its details exactly. The graceful old sink and tub, the hideous orange linoleum, the bright green walls. And the rest of that apartment too. The drab stubby carpet we never vacuumed and I begged him to let me rip out, the lumpy old couch that we took from his parents' basement– and in his eyes every time he looked at it I saw his lament for the white leather sectional his ex-wife had "stole"– our lazy depressing poverty that made no sense and its resulting and perpetual hysteria. The little old lady on the brink of death downstairs. She watched soaps all day, her TV on full blast while I slept, the restless flipping of the channels her only sign of life, so that even my dreams were infested with embarrassing clichés.

The lawyer's bill arrived. $3800 due on receipt. Fresh despair. The injustice! The suffering! We rushed to the bar with renewed and purposeful misery. Our local bar was cold and brown, with a smell that was almost clean, like layers of dry white ash compressed on one another. It recaptured perfectly the dives I'd passed in childhood, when I'd paused to inhale the mysterious blackness under the smell of stale beer and to hear the dull thud of glasses landing and occasional coughs that drifted out the unmarked door, sounds and smells of a relaxing human failure that drew me as a child.

Jake and I went to the bar every night and ate hamburgers and french fries and drank until we had no cash: usually Wednesday. He considered himself a local legend and always burst into the bar with his arms spread wide. He didn't notice nobody responded. My first drink dulled the shame of living with a laughingstock. Its almost unbearable sweetness numbed first my tongue, then the roof of my mouth and finally my brain. By the time he started crying I was no longer embarrassed.

At home we smoked bad pot and sat in front of an ancient TV eating more junk.

When stoned he managed to say exactly what I dreaded most. I'm just like McGyver, baby, don't you think? I told him he embarrassed me, I'd prefer it if he didn't speak, and he said that one day I'd betray him, all women were the same, nobody saw what he was offering, in the meantime he would be my teacher. When being serious he sounded like a mixture of Conan the Barbarian and Jesus Christ delivering the sermon on the mount. But every now and then his face looked puzzled. Why are you here with me, baby, if you hate me so much? And the meaty face across from mine was suddenly transformed. It saw me. For a moment I was terrified but then I saw that his insightfulness was just a fluke, his timing accidental, his face went on transforming, and later he again predicted I'd betray him before the cock crowed thrice. He was a stupid, stupid man.

A sordid fact I wanted to conceal. I'd stay forever to conceal it.

And so we lay awake at night, side by side, grinding our teeth in despair.

In winter, when the restraining order finally

expired, he was allowed to collect his things from the ex-wife. I wanted a look at the mercifully lost vibrating couch and the ex- wife in the glory of three hundred extra tax-free dollars every week, but again he would not let me come. He had one thing to be proud of, me, but I no longer argued with him.

He and Bob Wickett left in the afternoon and returned at three a.m., when I was stationed in the window where I always sat and waited for his truck- he often staggered home at three a.m.- lurching up the stairs with a large musty cardboard box.

"Baby, I present you my balls," he said.

A framed poster of Conan the Barbarian. Boob-shaped salt and pepper shakers.

His class ring. A mirror with his high school mascot, a blue chicken, painted in the middle. In the morning they went on display.

I sank a little lower into my exhausted shame.

The heightened, ridiculous state of crisis never faded.

But ten dollars could buy enough cheap drugs to keep me awake for three days straight. The exact chemical makeup of what we snorted remained a frightening mystery but it felt like Ajax burning deep inside my brain. We bought from a couple named Phil and Kathy, who lived with six sullen blond children in a mobile home outside of town. Kathy was obsessed with laundry and their place smelled fresh but chemical and was always hot and humid. She had a heavy sagging face and stiff blonde hair but thick translucent skin that was pleasantly pale and she wore T-shirts that were blinding white. Phil was always rolling joints. They seemed to hardly notice us. But my shame for Jake was automatic, a constant feeling of impending doom, and I was too embarrassed by him to suspect their lethargy was drug-induced.

"I practically raised Phil here, baby. Practically raised half the kids in his family. Remember, buddy? When my old man was still a cop? Phil here was at our house every day. I showed him the ways of the world, so to speak. Demonstrated how to handle the fair sex, if you capture my drift."

There was a long pause while Phil finished a joint and laid it slowly in the box and finally looked up. In his face I always saw contempt.

"Sure did, my man. Sure did."

"Practically raised half the kids in his family."

Another long pause and then: "you're the man. You are most surely the man."

"Those were some days. Those were really some days, were they not?"

I closed my eyes against the tender swelling shame and wished we'd get the drugs and leave. Jake stood hunched around his can of beer, unsure how to hold his new fat body– without the cocaine he had gained fifty pounds. Finally he cleared his throat. This was apparently a sign, because Kathy sighed and got up from the table and Jake followed her slowly down the hall, leaving me alone with Phil. He continued rolling joints as if I wasn't there but now and then he laughed at nothing, laughter that took a few seconds coming, like a bubble rising to the surface of a tub, then burst in my face with aggressive indifference. I had the feeling he wanted to say something to me. Every few minutes a child peeked around the corner slowly. Then Jake returned, stuffing a small white envelope into the front pocket of his tight jeans, his fingers jammed in his pocket, his belly peeking out beneath his untucked shirt.

"We're mighty grateful for your fine hospitality,"

Jake always said in the squeaky voice he used when he felt vulnerable, and with a sheepish grin he rocked on his heels.

Back in the truck he reminded me that Kathy was a lesbian.

I pretended not to hear and finally refused to go on the drug runs with him and made him go alone. Whenever we drove past their mobile home he beeped the horn once, glanced at himself in the rearview mirror, and waved, though there was never anybody in the yard to see us passing. Always exactly the same.

Our every habit had become an ordeal.

Every month or so, when we were high, something happened to remind him of his daughter, Tracy. Sentimental tears welled in his eyes while he ground his teeth and talked about his "miracle baby," born with her guts outside her body, along with others genetic misfortunes that explained her continuous dazed smile. The next day he would buy something expensive and take it to his parents, who had agreed to raise her. Tracy's room smelled like piss and was already crowded with unused equipment. She knew the sound of his truck and always met us in the yard, where she jumped up and down and clapped, shouting

"Daddy! Daddy!" On one trip he made a big show of giving her his class ring, but she was only interested in pictures of prom dresses in teen magazines. The walls of her room were covered with them.

And yet these expeditions were a high point. I could not exactly say I liked his parents, but I liked their house. It was incongruously solid and built at the top of a large wooded hill, where it was almost like the wilderness. Behind the house there was a swimming pool, a bathhouse and a tennis court, all pleasantly gone to seed but functional. Inside the house was cool and smelled like firewood. There was restraint here. Decorum. Even if within this atmosphere of rugged wealth his parents themselves remained ridiculous, slightly off kilter.

Jake's mother was a shrewd and thrifty woman who'd worked fifty years in a rat- breeding factory. She was remarkably ugly even at 65, when things usually equalize. Her face was flat and rectangular, like a road sign covered in thin bluish skin, her mouth so small that she seemed to have difficulty eating, her legs like duffel bags. Jake's father was a former cop who had "retired" mysteriously. Hard transparent hairs grew out of his fat red bitter face and his stomach was dotted with strange blue lumps he made no effort to conceal. Three heart attacks had left him with a misleading saintly glow.

I sat with them by the pool, watching leaves that floated on its surface.

They were both a great deal smarter than their son, which unsettled me. I was never able to forget their blank surprise when they first saw me. Why, she's just a girl. They knew that my position was absurd. They knew it was all a mistake. They knew we were on drugs, and cheap drugs, too. They subtly tried to ask what I was doing. Did my parents know where I was? Had I considered college? I was terrified they knew how much I hated him, the thought of their knowing made my heart pound, I would rather stay forever than let them know about my hatred. So I pretended not to understand what they were asking me.

The truck rose over the crest of the hill and for an instant I was blinded by the sun. Then just as quickly everything was clear. The valley, if you could call it that, was a brilliant yellowy green that turned my stomach. The air outside was dead, rubber with humidity, and the heat did not feel natural. The open window was like a heat duct on full blast.

As we gained speed, coasting down the hill to where the sun would set, I tried to freeze my vision on one place long enough to look into the dark recesses of the woods that lined the road. I wished I had a cold glossy leaf in my hand, something I could peel apart in sections. I'd once put a particularly wide healthy specimen of leaf into my mouth, expecting it to be tasteless, but instead it was sharp and medicinal like ear wax, a taste that spread across my tongue and sank like ink saturating newsprint.

I was attracted by the trees, and sometimes tried to walk in them. I looked out the window of his parents' kitchen with its thick clear piece of plastic on the table dotted with burn holes, the smell of weak brewed coffee like a church, then got up without a word and went outside. But like everything here the woods disappointed me. The dry sticks prodded my ankles, the heat bore down through the holes in the stagnant leafy ceiling, in a clearing it actually sang, there was a constant groan and snap of insects. I wanted a drink and sometimes I even thought ahead and brought one with me. The ice hissed and cracked while I walked and the wet glass kept sliding through my hand. The whiskey produced an oppressive sweetness in my head but nothing else, no point of release from myself and wherever I walked the house was always right behind me.

We were passing Phil and Kathy's. He tapped the horn with his fist and absently waved, brushing his hair back with his palm as usual. His jaw dangled open and I could see his dry porous tongue poised at the bottom of his shrunken front teeth and the two rows of blackened fillings and the lake of spit the body of his tongue was floating on. He could not look away from himself. The tongue probed gently between his teeth and then reeled back and dabbed the corner of his mouth and he looked deep into his own eyes in the rearview, intensely pleased and absorbed, as if at a photo that captured him just as he liked to imagine himself: plaintively glum and sensitive, like an idiotic Kerouac. A thin shining line of snot slid from his nose like something alive and he stopped it with his tongue.

"You're not going to be like this around your parents, are you?" I said.

"My parents?"

I glanced across the seat at him. My toes felt cramped inside their shoes. He was a huge white bulk beside me. A bright white shirt with a stiff flaring collar that extended to his sloping shoulders and had plastic inserts that held different shapes like chicken wire. One up, one down. It was an embarrassing shirt, disco, a genuine piece: twenty years old and incredibly vulgar. And he had selected it specifically to please me. To keep me from leaving. But he was distraught and overlooked details. He never pulled it down across his belly or tucked it in and half the fabric was bunched around his shoulders. He appeared to be leaning forward, clinging to the steering wheel with all his might, but it was only the shirt that made him look that way: the shirt and his belly. He turned to face me and everything moved except his eyes, which stayed glued to themselves in the mirror.

"I'm not a bad-looking guy, am I, baby?"

I said nothing and finally he tore his eyes loose and turned them to me too.

"What do my parents have to do with anything?"

"Jesus." I looked away. A sneer was tugging at my mouth as tangible as fingers.

"Just try to stay calm around them if you can. Don't tell them anything."

I was looking, as if calmly, out the window. There was a promise hidden in what I'd said– behave well and I might not leave– but I knew he didn't hear it and was glad.

"This is a horrible place," I said, aware that my voice was annoyingly pretentious. "It's impossible for me to live here anymore."

I was pretentious with him all the time. I could say anything I wanted– I could say I was a communist once- I knew people in the music business when I was in New York– and he never knew the difference. I'd become terribly lazy. I could feel him tugging, like a child, on my arm: he pinched my skin between his fingers.

"Oh, baby, don't you see, it doesn't matter. Why can't you just accept things?"

It was the squeaky voice. I felt a morbid curiosity and turned to look at his face. It was still aimed straight at me and tears had swelled in his eyes and hung there, wavering, by a supernatural force. His face looked too precise and round, almost lewd in the bright afternoon light. Trees were flashing by behind his head and he was grimacing absurdly. I hated him in such a physical way that it was hard for me to speak.

"What does that mean?" I said.

"That comment strikes me as meaningless."

"Don't you see? You need to accept. Nothing can be that important, baby. You need to accept. Accept that I'm leaving. I want to be alone."

My voice sounded twice as loud as his. Was I shouting? My finger tapped steadily, quickly on my warm bare thigh, as if I was already somewhere else, as if it was over and I was waiting in a office somewhere.

"You're gonna—" his voice cracked; his expression turned pleading. He grabbed my tapping finger and twisted it into his cold slippery palm. "You're gonna go straight to that guy, I know it. I'll kill the scrawny little bastard!"

The sneer took hold of my face again and my breath was cold on my lips. I had been thinking of someone else, but that was just coincidence. I would not go from one to another. It was true that my thoughts strayed to another man's dank little face, and this other face was radiant when I appeared outside his door. He was flushed and panting, as if he'd just been exercising. He was the only one who ever asked me directly: how can you be with that guy? Eww. My hands were clasped on a plain warm cup and I answered earnestly, if not with the truth: I get used to the idea, then suddenly it shocks me again. Two years. But I've made promises and now I have to honor them. Promises? Honor? he echoed with a dry pompous laugh. He's human, I added. Oh, I see: he's human. When he was sarcastic his lips grew fuller, like a woman's. He also had a woman's body. A fleshy upturned butt, wide hips. After a pause I told him that Jake used to be thin. I said he was really different thin.

It didn't matter so much that he was stupid, I said, when he was physically intact and had a rugged charm.

"I know exactly what you are," Jake said.

He was pressing my wrist into the seat. But his hand was slippery and could hardly keep its hold.

I closed my eyes and the lids glowed pale red and my mouth felt spacious. He won't let me leave, I thought. But he would let me leave, of course. I would only have to endure the talking first. And his parents' disappointment. I could feel the truck struggling up a hill and sluggishly opened my eyes, but I saw we were still at the bottom of the valley, not going up a hill at all. We passed through a tunnel of old maples, tapped for syrup and dotted with white plastic buckets.

"All woman are the same and you'll run straight to him."

"As usual you're wrong. Not every one is so pathetic."

I was irreproachable. I had never lied. I had never so much as touched the other one. But I could not help thinking about his damp brick house– such a small house among such big houses, on the only fancy street in town, and totally bare inside. If I did go to him it would be only for a minute, because I was so tired. To rest. To get a ride somewhere. To be with somebody unknown. Someone who would never wear a shirt like that, at least. To be away from myself. Or no. Not at all. Of course I couldn't go at all.

"If you think —."

If you think I'm leaving you for someone else

then you're deluded, was what I'd planned to say. But only the first three words came out. The shirt was glowing next to me. I'd lit a cigarette. I could not remember doing this but there it was, perched between my stiff red knuckles, slightly bent, and twirling off too much smoke as if it wasn't burning right. Through the smoke his face was clearer than ever, grinning now.

"Fuck think. I need not think," he said. "I know. Am I not familiar with women by now, after they've all fucked me? Do I not know that woman are all the same and you're a woman too, you pretend to be different but you are a typical cunt. Typical."

I turned my face away, laughing, and sucked hard on the cigarette. I understood his reference: he was talking about my sexual tastes. An hour earlier, when he was crying into the cheap metal sink in our kitchen, I'd watched his shaking hairy back and suddenly remembered something and smiled almost joyously. If you want me so much, I said, then seduce me. Make me stay. When he turned around his face was puckered and deflated. You typical cunt, he said. Now you think you've threatened me, so I'll perform.

"I've never betrayed you," I said.

"And I'm trying to be honest. I think you owe me more than this."

"Honest? You're trying to be honest?" he said. The absurd grimace returned and he shook a fist at me. "This is what I owe you."

He rattled the fist again, then turned and punched the windshield. For an moment nothing happened. The truck was floating through the valley. Then the windshield slowly started to crack and suddenly it shattered all at once. I put out my hands and waited for it to crumble into our laps. But the thing adhered to itself. It hung pouched in front of us while we skidded to the side of the road. He'd just stopped paying his insurance and I was thinking how much this would cost to repair. As if it was still my concern.

I looked at his belly and at the fist nuzzled into his lap and noticed his class ring.

"My god," I said. "Did you take that thing back from Tracy?"

And when he didn't answer– he was crying– I added: "You couldn't have done it without a ring, you think I don't know that? You think I'm impressed?"

When we finally rolled into his parents' driveway he seemed excited about something, an undercurrent of manic jubilance in his eyes.

He made us drinks and put on music, Indigo Girls of all things, then went into their bathroom. His parents weren't even home. He'd dragged me out here, knowing they were an effective threat, to perform the grand finale of our sexual misunderstanding: they were out of town.

He came out of the bathroom in shiny leather pants and a black leather vest with no shirt underneath. Not a flattering ensemble. He circled me slowly with his horrifying smile and introduced himself as "Jake."

He said he was new around here and his bike was parked outside and he wondered if he could buy me a drink. It took me a moment to grasp what he was doing and then I closed my eyes with shame and hateful pity. If it was degradation that I wanted, I had certainly succeeded.

But he couldn't think of anything more to say and circled around me, grinning, until I could no longer stand it and threw my drink on the floor. It landed on the carpet with a hollow thud and cracked open like an egg.

"You idiot!" I said. "It has to be something real. Go down to the bar and bring them back, charge them twenty dollars each, I don't care, but do something."

I watched his expression turn inside out. The smile became the baleful shriveled expression of a salivating man about to vomit and then he ran out of the room in tears.

Later we "borrowed" his father's old red Cadillac and forty dollars and went to the bar, though it was almost closing time. We stopped as we usually did to get Bob Wickett, whose car had been repossessed. He said nothing about the Cadillac but slid into the front seat next to me as if we were driving the truck. Wedged between them, I was aware of a strange sour smell coming from between my legs.

The bar was already dark. The only light came from a string of colored bulbs around the mirror where the bartender, an obese asthmatic old woman called Corky, shuffled back and forth restocking bottles, now and then stopping to make a panicked sucking through her nose. The jukebox clicked and whirred but played no music. Click. Whir. Jake went to ask for a drink. We were not alone. There were the usual slouched defeated backs along the bar. The usual pair of women in the corner with big elaborate hair, leaning against each other, drunk and startled-looking. And something unusual too. Phil and Kathy were walking toward our table. I hadn't seen them in a year.

Phil had lost much of his hair. I could not take my eyes off his expanded forehead. Kathy was not prospering either. Frizz hung in two dead flaps on the side of her face like spaniel ears, there were perfect dark circles around her eyes, her mouth hung open and her chin was slack. She wore nothing but a halter top and tight red shorts. A luminous expanse of flesh and she seemed to be freezing. Her teeth chattered inside clenched lips and she clutched her arms around her stomach but at the same time she was sweating. At the back of my muffled, drunken mind I suspected there was something wrong with her. A terminal condition not yet diagnosed. Jake came back with drinks for everyone. Our table was just big enough to hold the drinks and our faces hovered in a tense circle.

I was one drink beyond caring what this meant, I only knew that my escape was not going to succeed, that I would wake up in the morning next to him again.

"Whoo, let's party!" Kathy yelled suddenly.

She waved her heavy arms above her head and her breasts sloshed back and forth. Bob Wickett winced and sprang up from his chair, grabbed his drink and sauntered across the room toward the two drunk women in the corner. He was so bow-legged, and so habitually embarrassed, that he always seemed to saunter so he could arrive sideways.

He settled at their table with something like grace, he had a way of melting in, of immediately looking like he'd been there all along, sipping his drink and surveying the room nonchalantly. He had a protruding chin and forehead and his face folded in on itself like an overstuffed suitcase. His glasses slanted outward from the bottom of his eyes at so sharp an angle that even in the darkness they reflected glare. He was not interested in these women. They were much too old for him– he preferred prepubescent girls and every day walked the rounds of the convenience stores, drinking Mountains Dew and trying to pick up the girls who had dropped out of school to work as cashiers, at which even without a car he was alarming successful– he had only moved across the room from embarrassment. One of them had an unlit cigarette stuck between her lips and was pecking her head at him in hopes of a light.

Jake and Kathy suddenly got up and left the table too. They went to the bar and appeared to be having an argument. Phil was looking for something on the floor. His bald patch, the shape of India upside down, was staring me straight in the face. The jukebox came on but before I recognized the song it took a slow mournful dive. The last drugged note went on ten seconds and the machine thumped once and then was silent and I could hear their voices at the bar. Phil sat up and smiled at me. I picked up my drink and smiled back.

"I hardly recognized you," he said. "You've gotten fat."

The smile was frozen on my face and I felt suddenly, uneasily sober.

"I have?" I said involuntarily.

"The last time I saw you I thought you were hot. But now you're fat."

I glanced down at my lap and saw the flesh of my thighs spread on the metal seat. A small feeling of horror detached itself and began to float aimlessly around my brain. I looked up at him again and cleared my throat.

"I hardly know you," I said. "Why are you saying this?"

"Why not?" he said. "Jake didn't tell me that you spent the last year eating."

I took a sip of my drink and cleared my throat again. "Well, you've gone bald."

"Ha! That's a good one, that's a good one, you conceited bitch."

He tilted his beer and furiously sucked. His throat pulsated.

"Why," he said leaning forward, "are all women such fat pigs?"

He leaned back and absently traced the mouth of the bottle with his tongue. I was distracted by the flesh of my thighs on the seat. It took all my effort not to focus on it. I glanced at Jake and Kathy at the bar. They were still in a heated debate.

"No, really, I want to know," he said. "I've

always wondered why. Why don't you answer me? We're just talking. Don't you wonder why we're here tonight? I don't normally frequent this dump. You don't wonder? OK, I'll tell you. We're here because Jake called me earlier, from his old man's. He asked me to do him a favor. And tell you the truth, I think he was crying."

He sat forward and winked and looked over the edge of the table at my thighs.

"Do you know why he called? Hmm? Yes? No? Indifferent? Why won't you answer me? OK, OK, I'll tell you. You'll love it. So Jake calls me up tonight, and like I said I think he's crying, and–"

His face broke into a smile and he took a few long drinks.

"I'm sorry, I'm sorry, it's just so funny. Anyway he tells me that you need someone to fuck you. Can you believe it? He starts begging me to fuck you. Pretty motherfucking sad, if I must say so myself. I tell him, hey, for you old man, the sky's the limit, it's the least I can do, I tell him, since you practically raised me. He neglected to mention you were fat. But a promise is a promise, I'm a man of God, and I guess I'll fuck you anyway."

Again he traced the mouth of the bottle with his narrow tongue, and laughed.

"You know I sometimes handcuff Kathy inside the closet all day, and then when I come home I still don't want her! How can she be such a fat pig if she's handcuffed in the closet all day long? I really wish you would explain that to me. Damn."

I stood up carefully but knocked my chair to the floor, where it landed with a complicated clang. I left it there, turned, and started walking toward the bathroom. In the bathroom I locked the door and ran the water in the sink. I washed off my face and looked in the mirror. I'd selected the wrong moron. I stood on the toilet and craned for a look at my ass and the backs of my thighs. Then I took off my shirt and my shorts and climbed back on the toilet and examined myself again. How fat was I? It was impossible to tell. I noticed my drink, almost full, perched on the edge of the sink. Old friend! It had somehow made the journey with me. Clutching it, in my bra and underwear, I sank into a crouch between the toilet and the sink, so that my eyes were almost level with the toilet seat. A few of the tiles were loose and slipped beneath me with a snap. There was a flytrap hanging just above my head, heavy with flies and swaying like a pendulum: I must have touched it on the way down. The water was still running in the sink and I watched a steady leak in the pipe. Water fell onto a rotten spot in the floor and I hugged my knees and felt peaceful and hoped that nobody would need the bathroom. I started thinking about what Phil had said. I realized I would go with him. Why not? Yes, why not? In just a moment I would get up and go. But for now I felt so comfortable. It was hard for me to move.

When I finally emerged from the bathroom the room had been cleared and the lights turned back on. Bob Wickett was sitting at the bar. He saw me come out but he pretended not to and I went straight outside, looking for Phil.

It was raining and the air was hot and dense and still. I stood beneath the wide overhang of the squat flat roof. Water spattered in the muddy parking lot. A solid noise. Porous and full. There were still a few cars in the lot, belonging to people too drunk to drive home even by Michigan standards. I held out my hands as far as I could but they were still dry and I let them fall and stood for a moment with my mind blank and listened to the rain. I slowly understood the magnitude of my confusion: I was here and no where else, I hated instead of loving, I was trapped, but what did any of it matter? It was only a shadow of what was actually happening, someplace else, a fact that came to me sometimes, whole and complete, but then floated from my mind without a trace. I was exchanging awareness for weight. Thirty pounds gained slowly and unnoticed over time. That was how it happened. A faint light from an approaching car had fallen on the road and grew stronger until I saw the raindrops falling through it and then a huge sedan appeared, moving very slowly in the downpour. In this suspended moment of light the windshields of all the cars in the parking lot glowed, and in the red Cadillac I clearly saw two heads in a passionate embrace.

The car passed on; the two heads disappeared; they seemed to sink below the surface of the night. But I was smiling. Because I knew that it was Jake and Kathy.

Freedom! I had seen them. He was cheating. I was free. I stood there another minute and then went back inside and sat down next to Bob.

"You saw them, didn't you?" he moaned.

He took off his glasses, folded them, rubbed his eyes, and put them back on. Melodramas embarrassed him.

"Oh yeah, I saw them." I could not wipe the joyous smile off my face.

"I want you to know one thing. Kathy is a pig woman. I want you to know where I stand on this. You don't know how many times I've told him so. How many times I've asked him why, when he's got a fine piece like you at home so... young... and so quiet...."

"It's all right, Bob, look at me, I'm not upset."

The glasses were off again and his face, now that he was sure I wouldn't make a scene, was transformed by sympathy. He looked like a regular adult. I felt a pang for him.

"Those two are downright embarrassing," he said. "I want you to know that."

When Jake knocks on my door and I come out and I see his stupid grin and know she's in the truck– I feel like turning right around and going back inside."

"But listen, Bob – how fat have I gotten?"

He looked away and Corky set a drink in front of me and squeezed my arm. I took a satisfied sip– a free drink is a free drink– and then began to feel a suspicious.

"Wait a minute. Why does Corky feel sorry for me? They go ... out?"

The glasses were back on. He wouldn't look at me.

"Oh, well, it was a big scene. It was a regular bar brawl. Tables flying, people running for cover. It's her or me, Jake! Her or me! You better choose! I tell you, that woman should have been a prizefighter. A pig women. He had to sneak up from behind and drag her out kicking and screaming. I don't get it. When he's got a prime young thing like you at home. And smart too. Some dignity. And so young. A fine vocabulary. I hope you don't mind my saying that. And the way his old man sits there laughing with her, cursing up a storm like they're a couple of old sailors."

"You mean his father?" I said.

"Do you mean she goes to see his parents?"

Bob's embarrassed eyes had shifted to the door, where Jake stood with his horrifying sheepish smile. When I saw him I started to laugh again and remembered I was free.

Kathy was surprised by my tolerant attitude and kept declaring I was good people.

We were sitting at the kitchen table. She took tiny green pills from a prescription bottle while she talked and wiped her face with pink tissues. I was trying to assess her risk of infectious disease. It was nearly dawn but she was still unburdening herself on me, describing her suffering with Phil, he was a monster, he beat her up for no apparent reason, she showed me the bruises to prove it and I patted her hand and blandly assured her that was over. Good people, she said.

"Jake would take care of her now," I said.

She sighed, "Such good people."

She talked about all the men who wanted her and then about Jake. We would like to buy a house, she said. We would like to have a child.

"What about the dozen children already have? And have you seen Tracy?"

Jake observed us, grinning like a talk show host who's just united long-lost sisters, refilling our glasses from a jug of cheap red wine which in ignorance we kept refrigerated. Just a few more hours, I told myself. The kitchen was bright lemon yellow. Lightning flashed outside, I could see the trees, for a moment I was worried about the Cadillac, but then I remembered it was their problem now. She finally ran out of things to say and started yawning. I insisted that she and Jake take the bed.

Good people. Such good people.

I lay on the scratchy couch in the dark and looked at the paper window shade.

After a few minutes, as I expected, Jake crept into the living room.

"Baby," he whispered desperately. "Does this mean you understand?"

"Get her out of here tomorrow so I can pack my things and leave."

"No, baby, you don't understand, she needed me, I went over there one night and she was masturbating right there on the couch and it was so sad and I was just--"

"Shut up. You're an idiot. Get out of here. I'm tired."

I was grinning in the darkness. What a relief to be justified, to shed my ambiguity.

And what a joy to say these words, so icily, at last.

"Go on, get out, I want to get some sleep."

His shape obediently disappeared from the door. The room was empty of all but the long, bulky shape of the couch I lay on and the old TV in the corner on the floor which was definitely not top-of-the-line. The couch was hard and lumpy. The springs were fighting through the fabric. I went to the kitchen for a glass of water. A slow distant drumbeat in my head signaled an approaching hangover. I saw the light was on in the bedroom and on my way back I paused at the sliver of light and closed one eye. I watched Jake, naked, his penis fully erect, playfully flick an unfamiliar towel at Kathy's thick, shiny, contorted body with its heavy breasts and the tall upward-turning horn of hair between her legs and two square buttocks spotted with bruises until they fell together with a sharp creak on the bed.

I returned to the couch and strained to hear the noises from the bedroom. But all I could hear was the old refrigerator humming in the kitchen. Every few minutes tires swished through puddles on the road outside. How hard it was going to be, to start a new life not only hungover and broke but fat too. I got up for another glass of water. Now the light was off. I stood by the bedroom door and pushed it open silently.

The room was bright from a streetlamp by the

window and they were asleep, not touching, pale and mammoth, on top of the tattered bedspread. I took a few steps toward them. The unfamiliar towel was pulled tight between her legs and there was a dark stain between them on the bedspread. Was I as fat as she was? I suddenly remembered my first day here with Jake, when I wasn't fat at all. It was early in the morning but already very hot and he left the room to see about his job and get a lawyer. I suspected he was both hiding me and showing me off and that was just what I wanted. I was just playacting. I went to the motel's office and I knew the man behind the desk was watching me and wondering what I was doing here and so I lingered, pretending to look at the maps and coupon books until he'd had a good look and I went slowly to my room and got into the clean white bed, not sure Jake would ever be back and not exactly caring either. Somebody would come, if not Jake then somebody else. There was too much certainty in the white motel-smelling sheets for me to be disappointed long.

I noticed a pair of glistening, black-rimmed eyes: Kathy was awake.

I backed quickly out of the room and sat on the couch again. There was a distinct light on the window shade now and more cars were passing outside. People were on their way to work. That seemed funny to me: normality reasserting itself. The rain had started to fall again and my hangover was getting closer. They were arguing in the bedroom. Then Kathy appeared in the doorway. It was even lighter than I'd realized and I could see her clearly. She was wearing my bathrobe.

"Now I know why you were nice to me," she said.

"And why is that?"

"You wanted something."

I could hear Jake slapping around barefoot in the kitchen. He opened the refrigerator, spreading a faint yellow light. I noted with relief that the bathrobe didn't close on her. A two-inch stripe of her body was exposed. Jake bit into something hard.

"Listen sweetheart," she said, "drop the shit.

He told me all about it, he's been telling me for months... that you want to get in bed with us. And I was plenty pissed, believe me. I said, I'll show the little cunt. But Jake calmed me down and I remembered you were nice to me and so I'm out here telling you real sweet. We're not into that. You got it?"

The window shade was getting lighter as she talked.

"Got it. You can keep the bathrobe," I said,

"It looks good on you."

ABOUT the AUTHOR

Kristin Hart is the University Dean of Libraries and Information Resources at The City University of New York (C.U.N.Y.) She has been Chief Librarian and Associate Dean at Queens College, Flushing, NY, and Library Director of The Maritime College of the State University of New York (S.U.N.Y.), and Adelphi University Manhattan Center Librarian.

Her publications include *Collecting and Using Data to Inform Space Design; Emerging Scholars* and *Alternative Search Platforms: Using Game Theory to Understand Searching Behavior.*

She is a Digital Culture grant recipient from the Metro Organization and writes a monthly Op-Ed Column, which has appeared in *D News; The Knight News* and *The Riverdale Press.*

ABOUT the PRESS

Washington Street Press is the straightforward of the two imprints published by eMediaLoft.org, issuing fiction, non-fiction, and monographs. The other, Xanadu Press, produces books in which pictures and texts are imaginative and visually linked. Both are designed and edited by media artist and writer, Barbara Rosenthal. Her column of philosophy about the interconnection of art and artist, *A Crack in the Sidewalk,* appears in *Whitehot Magazine of Contemporary Art,* and her creative bookworks are in the collections of The Whitney, MoMA, Tate, Berlin Kunstbibliotek, et al. No submissions are accepted; publication is by invitation only.

eMediaLoft.org is located within the Westbeth Arts Complex on the Hudson River in the Highline area of NYC. It is a privately funded loose consortium of artists and others who create hard-to-place, hard-to-categorize works, primarily overlapping within replicable or recordable media: camera and electronic arts, performance and writing, with a strong conceptual base and discernible philosophical perspective.